SINCERELY, Harriet

SARAH WINIFRED SEARLE

Graphic Universe™ • Minneapolis

For the cool librarians of Kennebunk Free Library, who introduced this reluctant reader to a broader world of graphic novels, zines, and other books that felt like they were made just for her

Graphic Universe™
A division of Lerner Publishing Group, Inc.
241 First Avenue North
Minneapolis, MN 55401 USA

For reading levels and more information, look up this title at www.lernerbooks.com.

Library of Congress Cataloging-in-Publication Data

Names: Searle, Sarah Winifred, author, illustrator.
Title: Sincerely, Harriet / Sarah Winifred Searle.
Description: Minneapolis : Graphic Universe, [2019] | Summary: In 1996 Chicago, thirteen-year-old Harriet Flores, living with boredom, loneliness, and a chronic illness, lets her imagination run wild—with mixed results—and learns about the power of storytelling.
Identifiers: LCCN 2018014447 (print) | LCCN 2018021004 (ebook) | ISBN 9781541542723 (eb pdf) | ISBN 9781512440195 (lb : alk. paper) | ISBN 9781541545298 (pb : alk. paper)
Subjects: LCSH: Graphic novels. | CYAC: Graphic novels. | Hispanic Americans—Fiction. | Imagination—Fiction. | Multiple sclerosis—Fiction.
Classification: LCC PZ7.7.S417 (ebook) | LCC PZ7.7.S417 Si 2019 (print) | DDC 741.5/973—dc23

LC record available at https://lccn.loc.gov/2018014447

Manufactured in the United States of America
1-42281-26138-9/14/2018

SHEDD aquarium CHICAGO

Hannah!
   Sorry I couldn't come to
camp this year, really wish I
could but we had to move to
Chicago. It's ok so far, kinda
weird not having a car. Today
we went to the aquarium! The
penguins are super cute. How
are you? How's camp? Is Ashley
there? Say hi for me. You have to
eat 100 burnt marshmallows in
my honor. Each. No cheating!
   ♡ Harriet

Hannah Baum
Pine Point Camp
1 Pine Point Rd
Greencrest, IN 46511

13

14

This works.

Hmm... where did I go today?

Dear Hanna

crrrreeeak

Did you remember to get more stamps?

Oh yeah!

Have you heard from your friends yet?

Thanks, Papa. Hope you have a good day.

Here's a thought. Why don't you go downstairs and pay Pearl a visit today?

I keep some treats around for the grandkids. Have as much as you like.

Thanks.

I'll select photos, then you'll paste them in and make sure they're nice and straight. Sound good?

Got it.

I'm putting this album together for my grandson.

So he always knows where his family comes from, and someday he can share it with his children.

But...do you want to know a secret?

Hmm?

I do it so I can try to remember better too.

ha ha

I can't recall their names for the life of me, and I thought my wedding was supposed to be the best day of my life.

Good thing it wasn't. If I'd hit the high point of my life at nineteen, I wouldn't have had much happiness left over for the next sixty years and counting.

28

Bleh.

Double bleh. Why did I ever try to like this stuff?

Brett dishes on his new rom-com role

TeenTown: So Brett, tell us about your new flick!

...amaville is about a ...misfit studer ...own ar

TeenTown: Mind sharing any juicy details of your award-nominated kiss with Winona?

Brett: (Laughs.) Cut to the chase, why don't ya!

Brett: She's so professional, I don't want to divulge too much. But I will say that she uses this fruity lip balm – cherry, maybe? – and I'll always remember her for it.

So, did you get some reading done today?

Yeah.

Harriet Alejandra. Tell the truth.

Okay, maybe I didn't, but Pearl needed my help with something and it took *all* afternoon!

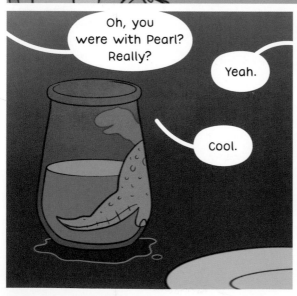

Oh, you were with Pearl? Really?

Yeah.

Cool.

How's she doing, anyway?

Fine, I guess. But I have my suspicions.

No one lives on the third floor, right? Haven't you wondered what's up there?

Storage?

I hear weird noises when I'm alone, and at night, and...what if...

What if something weird happened here? What if it's *haunted?*

Thank heavens that heat wave broke. Gorgeous day.

Is this one of Abuelita's tapes? What did she send this time?

Half an episode of that old puppet show and a couple music videos so far.

Nice.

41

Maybe the *ghost* wrote this.

So, how do you entertain yourself while your folks are at work?

Um...watch movies. Read some, too. I've got catching up to do before school starts.

What kind of reading?

Right now, *The Great Gatsby.*

Ah. Not a fan, I take it?

Eh. I know it's supposed to be important or something, but...

It doesn't feel like it was written for *me,* if that makes sense.

I know exactly what you mean.

You do?

I was a librarian before I retired, you know. Books are my business.

Now, let's see...

How about... ...a classic?

When you finish *Gatsby,* give this a try. You don't have to finish it if you really hate it.

But I think it could give us something interesting to talk about. What do you think?

I guess I'll check it out.

Um, I was wondering...what's on the third floor?

Storage.

No one's ever lived up there?

Well, yes, a long time ago. Not since my children moved out, though.

That's Nicholas, my eldest.

Dear Hannah,

How's camp so far? I miss flashlight tag and swimming and all that stuff, but we've been busy here, too. I made a friend, I bet you'd think he's _really_ cute. Why don't you and Ashley visit before school starts? We can all hang out together and Nick can show us some cool places around the city! ♡ Harriet

Hannah Baum

Pine Point Camp

1 Pine Point Rd

Greencrest, IN 46511

61

Mary Lennox has her flaws, yes. But that's part of what makes her story so satisfying.

She grows a lot over the course of the book.

Mm.

You didn't read it, did you?

You know, I brought this home for my Nicky when he was in quarantine.

Quarantine?

He came down with polio in '53 during the epidemic.

The hospital didn't have space for him, so we nursed him at home. He stayed up in his room on the third floor for about eight months.

Eight months?!

Ha ha. You know, now that I think of it, I don't think we cared much for this book.

Why would you give me something to read if you didn't like it?

Expecting something?

No.

Just thinking about that weird mailman.

What's weird about him?

Just a feeling. He's always creeping around people's houses...

Yes, so he can deliver their mail.

Have you seen the way he glares at the dogs across the street? It's like he's plotting something...*evil*.

Harriet...

I've known Gary Ganesh since he was born, and there isn't an ounce of cunning in that man.

He's nervous around dogs because the Jones's Chihuahua bit him when he was a kid. Almost lost his little finger.

Sorry if that's not much of a dark backstory, but if you enjoy the macabre, I could ask him to show you the scar.

N-no, that's okay.

Or, you know, you could write your *own* story about an evil mailman and make it as exciting as you want.

It gets easier with practice. Start with something you know.

Writing's *hard.*

Write about your life. See what happens.

Maybe.

My name is Harriet Alejandra Flores, I'm thirteen years old, and I hope we can be friends.

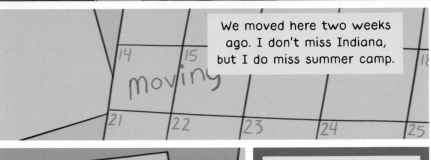

We moved here two weeks ago. I don't miss Indiana, but I do miss summer camp.

I understand why we needed to move here, but school doesn't start for almost another month, and I can't be at camp with Ashley and Hannah, and Mom and Papa are so busy with their new jobs when I just want to have a good summer, you know?

See, I've been homeschooled for the past two years. I had friends before, but we lost touch when I got sick. Camp was the first (and last) time I got to really hang out with other kids and have fun in forever.

I hope it's okay that I'm writing to you. I thought you might understand me.

Sincerely,

thd

Whew. Close one.

slp

thud!

Fine!

I mean, the usual, I guess. Yours?

Oh, the usual.

You've been quiet lately.

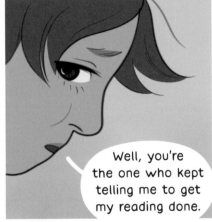

Well, you're the one who kept telling me to get my reading done.

I don't remember picking up that one at the library.

Pearl lent it to me.

Really? Cool.

Dear Nicholas,

I haven't heard from Hannah and Ashley yet. Do you think my postcards got lost? Maybe the weird mailman took them. Or the ghost in this house is hiding them.

Or maybe they're just too busy to write, I guess.

Hannah's always busy because she's friends with everyone ever. Her parents sent her lots of snacks and magazines that she always shared with our whole cabin, just because she's nice like that.

Ashley is Hannah's best friend. She's cool, too. Really cool.

She's tall, and good at everything, and she's quiet, but I kind of like that.

She gets sleepy when it's sunny out and can nap anywhere, like a cat. Her hair's a gold color that almost doesn't look real.

How about you, Nicholas? What are your friends like? Do they visit?

Is there someone you like?

TeenTown: Mind sharing any ju~~~ kiss
details of your award-nominated kiss
with Winona?

Brett: (Laughs.) Cut to the chase,
why don't ya!

She's so professional, I don't want
to divulge too much. But I w~~~
that she uses this fruity lip~~~
– cherry, maybe? – and I'll
remember her for it.

TeenTown: Any memorable s~~~
~~~ the set that you could

Dinner in five,
Harry! Can you help
set the table?

B-be right
there, Papa!

Sweet dreams.

You two seem pretty tuckered out. Did I miss some excitement?

Oh, nothing much, just a ragin' party. The whole neighborhood was here.

Darn.

sigh

So *that's* where the dumbwaiter goes.

So, what do you think of *To Kill a Mockingbird* so far?

It's, um...

...I haven't really started it yet. Sorry.

Well, let me know when you get there.

It's tough to get into books a lot of the time. I like movies better.

I suppose they're not all that different, are they? Just different ways to tell stories.

I'll always find it easier to lose myself in a good book more than anything else, but I can respect a good film.

Are there any that have stuck with you, Harriet?

I don't know.

Are there any stories that have lingered in your mind, even long after finishing them?

Yeah. I mean, it changes, but... *Beetlejuice,* maybe?

I don't...

How about this: Do you have a favorite?

I guess? I mean...I don't know.

I can see that. It's about a girl who moves into a weird old house, right? That must resonate with you about now.

It must be hard, being away from your friends. But school starts again in a few weeks, you'll meet new kids—

Stop.

You don't know me. You don't know *anything.*

Harriet—

I gotta go finish my chores.

She just doesn't get it.

rustle CLINK

97

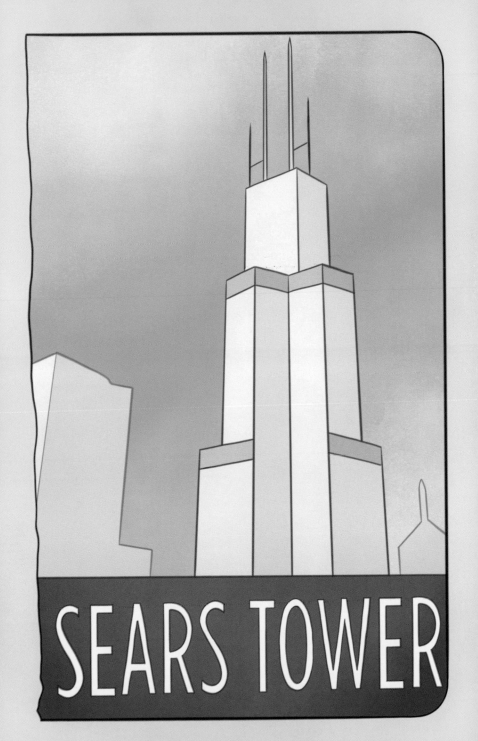

Your camp friends'll write back soon, I'm sure.
You'll see.
Yeah.

SEARS TOWER

Dear Hannah,

I'm going to be pretty busy for a while, so this is probably my last postcard for now, and you might want to put off any visits you were planning. Maybe after school starts. Anyway, I hope the rest of camp is fun.

Ta-Ta!

Sincerely,
Harriet

Hannah Baum

Pine Point Camp

1 Pine Point Rd

Greencrest, IN 46511

My boss agreed to let me out of overtime if I use it to finally finish my nursing degree. I start classes in a few weeks.

That's so great!

Congrats, hon.

Love you two so much!

Gross!

107

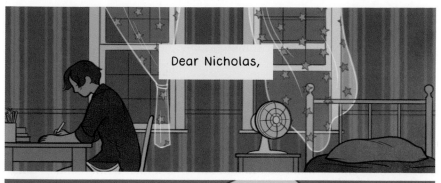

Dear Nicholas,

I probably owe you an apology. I'm sorry I haven't been 100% truthful with you...

But I think I lie to myself more than anyone else.

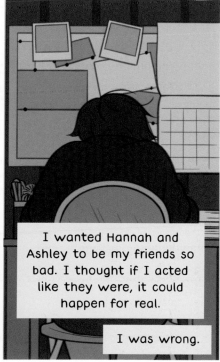

I wanted Hannah and Ashley to be my friends so bad. I thought if I acted like they were, it could happen for real.

I was wrong.

I'm only telling you this because you're not real. Or, well, you're real, but you'll never see this.

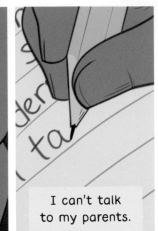

I can't talk to my parents.

They think I'm scared of being sick, but it's not really that. They don't understand, just like Pearl.

I think *you'd* understand, though.

I know it wouldn't be how I imagine it, but...

I wish we could meet.

115

117

Bad idea, Harriet.

This is a bad, bad idea, but...

Desperate times...

...call for desperate measures.

creeeak

Whew.

Hmph!

ssshhhhshhhh

Are you *sure* you feel all right? I can't believe you weren't seriously injured.

What on God's Earth were you doing, playing in that thing?

I... I don't know.

Your father told me about what's going on, what you've all been through. I offered to help keep an eye on you.

132

134

140

'But who is he, my —'

'He is Peter Pan, you know, mother.'

At first Mrs. Darling did not know, but after thinking back into her childhood she just remembered a Peter Pan who was said to live with the fairies. There were odd stories about him; as that when children died he went part of the way with them, so that they should not be frightened. She had believed in him at the time, but now that she was married and full of sense she quite doubted whether there was any such person.

'Besides,' she said to Wendy, 'he would be grown up by this time.'

'Oh no, he isn't grown up,' Wendy assured her confidently, 'and he is just my size.' She meant that he was her size in both mind and body; she didn't know how she knew it, she just knew it.

Mrs. Darling consulted Mr. Darling, but he smiled pooh-pooh. 'Mark my words,' he said, 'it is some nonsense Nana has been putting into their [...] just the sort of idea a dog would have. [...]

'Now, [...] replied [...] you please.' She made [...] by inclining her face toward [...] merely dropped an acorn butto[...] hand, so she slowly returned [...] where it had been before, a [...] that she would wear his [...] round her neck. It was [...] put it on that chain. [...] for it was afterwar[...] to save her life. [...]

...neck. It di[...] ...cky that she [...] ...it on that chain, ...for it was afterward... ...to save her life. ...When peop[...] ...ustomar[...] ...d so [...]

The A... ...uld be subli... ...ed across the wate... ...was to be heard a sound... ...musical and the most melancholy... world: the mermaids calling to the moo...

Peter was not quite like other boys; but he was afraid at last. A tremor ran through him, like a shudder passing over the sea; but on the sea one shudder follows another till there are hundreds of them, and Peter felt just the one. Next moment he was standing erect on the rock again, with that smile on his face and a drum beating within him. It was saying, 'To die will be an awfully big adventure!'

...Is this how you felt, Nicholas?

SSSSSshhhh

I don't want to feel like that.

I tried writing in the diary, but it didn't work. I want to talk for real.

We're here for you, honey.

You don't talk about it much, but I know you miss music.

And I don't want Papa to have to quit school again because of my MS.

Actually, Mom and I had a talk about that. If it comes to it, we'll work together better this time around so she can find a new band, and I can still do night classes.

I don't regret taking time off with you even a little, Harriet. And don't worry. This time, it really feels right to go back.

We're both going back to school in a few weeks, *together*.

Let's go supply shopping! How about you pick me out one of those sparkly zipper binders, so the other kids know I'm cool?

Really?

Heh, yeah.

Is there anything else on your mind?

What if I don't make any friends?

It might take some time to find the right people, but—

No, Mom. You don't get it.

148

I think his mind is full of more important things, now that he's in college.

It's the sort of gift that he'll appreciate more as he gets older.

And, after all, I also do this for myself.

These albums help me remember, but it's more than that. I can keep things the way I hope my family will remember them, too.

I'm curating our memories through these time capsules.

Is...is Nicholas's bedroom a time capsule, too? To lock away the bad memories?

Yes, that sounds about right. At least, that's how it was at first.

But now that Nicky's grown up with his own family, it's not as hard to think back on that time.

Sometimes I wonder if it was the best choice, but I think it helped us move on with our lives. To heal.

I think I get it.

But...why didn't you ever change it? Or get rid of that... that big metal thing?

I'm afraid this answer might disappoint you, but after so many years, I think we all just stopped thinking about it.

We occasionally discuss the future of this house, cleaning it out and remodeling, but for now, I'm content to leave it as is. My children will come home when they're ready, and we'll deal with it together.

These are *my* favorites.

I don't expect you to read all of these right now. Some you might have to grow into. But I want you to have them.

This is a movie, right?

Yes, it is. After you read it, we can have a movie night and see which holds up better.

These books will challenge you, but it's worth it.

And maybe you'll find something here to inspire stories of your own.

Yeah.

You could even write *movies.* I'd love to see a Harriet Flores picture someday.

Really?

Truly.

Hey, so, Pearl suggested I swing by the library today.

Looks like there's a creative writing group on Thursday afternoons. Would you like to go?

CREATIVE WRITING!

Can I?!

Well, yeah.

This house doesn't need any more ghosts.

Goodbye,
Ashley.

U-um, sorry—

Thanks.

Mm.

Harriet Alejandra's
☆ scrapbook ☆

Me as a baby! I was so cute, what happened?

1983

My parents before they had me! Mom said Papa made merch for her band and that's how they met.

He says they're "straight edge" whatever that is

Fluffy was
the best! I
miss him.

Summer camp
1995

Halloween
1995

We moved away in July 1996. Good bye, Indiana!

Chicago's okay, it has penguins

Abuelita even visited!

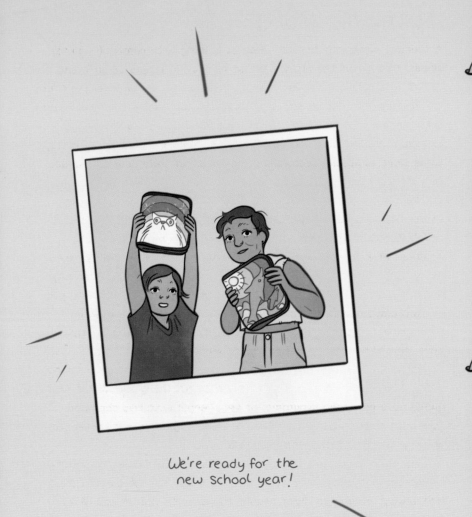

We're ready for the
new school year!

Author's Note

A theme I wove into *Sincerely, Harriet* is living with chronic (ongoing) illness. Throughout the story, I aimed to show a couple of different experiences people might have with it. Harriet has multiple sclerosis, or MS, a disease of the central nervous system. It affects communication between the brain and the rest of the body. In choosing the story's setting, I decided that Harriet's family would have moved to a big city to be close to special doctors that can help her learn how to manage this lifelong condition.

Pearl's son Nicholas had polio, a disease that can cause muscle weakness, paralysis, or even death. The 1950s saw one of the worst polio epidemics (widespread outbreaks) in American history. Black Americans faced strict segregation (the separation of people by race). Many hospitals prioritized space for white children. Families like Nicky's would have faced challenges in getting the medical care they needed.

Nicholas's iron lung, which Harriet sees during her trip upstairs, would have helped him breathe while he recovered. Later, he would have learned how to move again using mobility aids such as a wheelchair, leg braces, and crutches. We don't meet Nicholas as an adult in *Sincerely, Harriet*, but I envisioned that the grown-up Nicholas would have post-polio syndrome, or PPS. People with this condition may have muscle weakness, difficulty breathing, and other challenges many years after recovering from polio.

MS and PPS can both be considered *invisible disabilities*, or medical conditions that affect a person's daily life—even though the condition isn't always obvious to other people. For example, Harriet and Nicky use mobility aids sometimes but not always. When someone with an invisible disability doesn't need an aid, other people may forget their different needs. But people like Harriet and Nicholas may still feel their illnesses even if we can't see them.

At the same time, if we asked Nicholas who he is, he'd tell us about his kids, his poodles, and his career as a sports journalist. Just like how Harriet would tell us she loves movies, cooking, and maybe even writing. Their disabilities deserve our consideration and respect, but they don't define who they are as people.

Further Reading

Disability in Kidlit: Honor Roll
http://disabilityinkidlit.com/honor-roll/
This list of books includes many different
stories about characters with disabilities.

What Is an Invisible Disability?—The Invisible Disabilities Association
https://invisibledisabilities.org/what-is-an-invisible-disability
This page from the Invisible Disabilities Association shares more about
how to define invisible disability.

Author Acknowledgments

Tremendous gratitude to the Associates of the Boston Public Library,
for the residency where this seed first began to take root; M, M, J,
and C, for sharing your experiences so generously and for holding me
accountable; the Graphic Novel Workshop at CCS, for pushing this little
story to its fullest potential; my agent, Jen, for teaching and protecting
me so well; my editor, Greg, for taking a chance on me, and the whole
team at Lerner, for making this book the best it can be; my comics
cohort, including Niki, Kori, Lora, Melanie, Ali, and so many more, for
the constant flow of inspiration, wisdom, and support; and my precious
family and friends all across the world, including my partner, David,
whose love and understanding sustain me every single day. Thank you.

About the Author

Sarah Winifred Searle originally hails from spooky New England but
currently lives in sunny Perth, Australia. She's known for graphic
memoirs and fiction inspired by history and the connections between
people. When she isn't writing and drawing comics, Sarah's favorite
things are planning Dungeons & Dragons adventures with her partner,
rainy days with their foster cats, and naming the lizards and bugs that
live in their garden. Find her at swinsea.com.